Stop Those Socks!

'Stop Those Socks!'
An original concept by Jill Atkins
© Jill Atkins

Illustrated by Marina Pessarrodona

Published by MAVERICK ARTS PUBLISHING LTD
Studio 11, City Business Centre, 6 Brighton Road,
Horsham, West Sussex, RH13 5BB
© Maverick Arts Publishing Limited August 2020
+44 (0)1403 256941

A CIP catalogue record for this book is available at the British Library.

ISBN 978-1-84886-690-4

www.maverickbooks.co.uk

Orange

This book is rated as: Orange Band (Guided Reading)
This story is mostly decodable at Letters and Sounds Phase 5.
Up to five non-decodable story words are included.

Stop Those Socks!

by Jill Atkins
illustrated by Marina Pessarrodona

Bert, the zoo keeper, lived in a little house next to the zoo.

One Saturday, he looked out of his window.

The sun was high in the sky and there was

a light breeze.

First, he fed the elephant and the monkey.

Then he fed the giraffe and the antelope.

Then he went to get his socks, his pants,
his scarf and his gloves.

He put them in the
washing machine.

Round and round went the washing.

At last, it finished.

Bert pegged the washing on the line.

Then he went back into his house.

'Time for my nap,' he thought.

He sat down in his best chair

and fell asleep.

Suddenly, Bert sat up.

Something had woken him.

"Whooo," went the wind.

It howled down the chimney.

It whistled through the cracks
in the window frame.

15

'I must get the washing in,' Bert thought.

'It must be dry by now.'

He hurried outside and went to the washing line. But there were only two socks.

"Oh no!" Bert cried. "The rest of my washing has disappeared!"

Whoosh!

A strong gust of wind lifted the socks into the air.

"Stop those socks!" Bert cried.

He tried to catch them.

He rushed here and there, looking for his washing. First, he looked all over his garden.

Then he looked in the street.

He looked everywhere, but

his washing had disappeared.

'Oh dear,' he thought. 'I will have
another look for my washing later.
It's time to feed the animals again.'

He opened the gate and went into the zoo.

Then he saw the crowds.

Some people were by the elephant pen and the monkey house.

Some people were by the giraffe field and the antelope meadow.

They were pointing and laughing.

Bert hurried towards them.

His scarf was wrapped round the elephant's trunk.

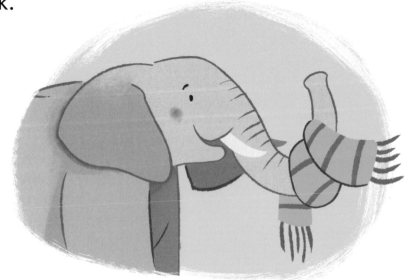

His pants were on the giraffe's head.

His gloves fitted the antelope's horns

perfectly.

And his socks were on the monkey's ears.

Bert laughed and laughed.

"They look so good," he said.

"They can keep my washing."

They all had fun on a windy day
at the zoo.

Quiz

1. What is Bert's job?
a) Farmer
b) Zoo keeper
c) Vet

2. Bert pegged the washing on the ____.
a) Tumble dryer
b) Line
c) Antelope

3. What happened to Bert's washing?
a) The animals took it
b) The rain made it wet
c) The wind lifted it into the air

4. Where did Bert find his lost washing?
a) In his garden
b) At home
c) At the zoo

5. What was on the monkey's ears?
a) Socks
b) Gloves
c) Hats

Turn over for answers

Book Bands for Guided Reading

The Institute of Education book banding system is a scale of colours that reflects the various levels of reading difficulty. The bands are assigned by taking into account the content, the language style, the layout and phonics. Word, phrase and sentence level work is also taken into consideration.

Maverick Early Readers are a bright, attractive range of books covering the pink to white bands. All of these books have been book banded for guided reading to the industry standard and edited by a leading educational consultant.

To view the whole Maverick Readers scheme, visit our website at

www.maverickearlyreaders.com

Or scan the QR code above to view our scheme instantly!

Quiz Answers: 1b, 2b, 3c, 4c, 5a